CONSERVATION FUND

My classmates and I enjoyed our day at SeaWorld sooo much, we decided to help all the animals in the ocean. Now you can, too.

The SeaWorld & Busch Gardens Conservation Fund donates to wildlife conservation projects around the world. They're helping study penguins in the Galapagos Islands and looking at where Pacific Loggerhead Sea Turtles go when they're swimming around Japan and following Right Whales in Florida.

SeaWorld and Busch Gardens parks are part of the Busch Entertainment Corporation, and they've been helping to conserve, rescue and study animals for more than 40 years. They have assisted more than 5,000 stranded, ill, orphaned or injured animals in the past ten years.

To find out more about this great way to help the animals of the world, visit swbg-conservationfund.org. All those coins really add up!

Herbert

SEAWORLD & BUSCH GARDENS CONSERVATION FUND

231 S. Bemiston Avenue, Suite 600, Clayton, MO 63105   www.swbg-conservation-fund.org

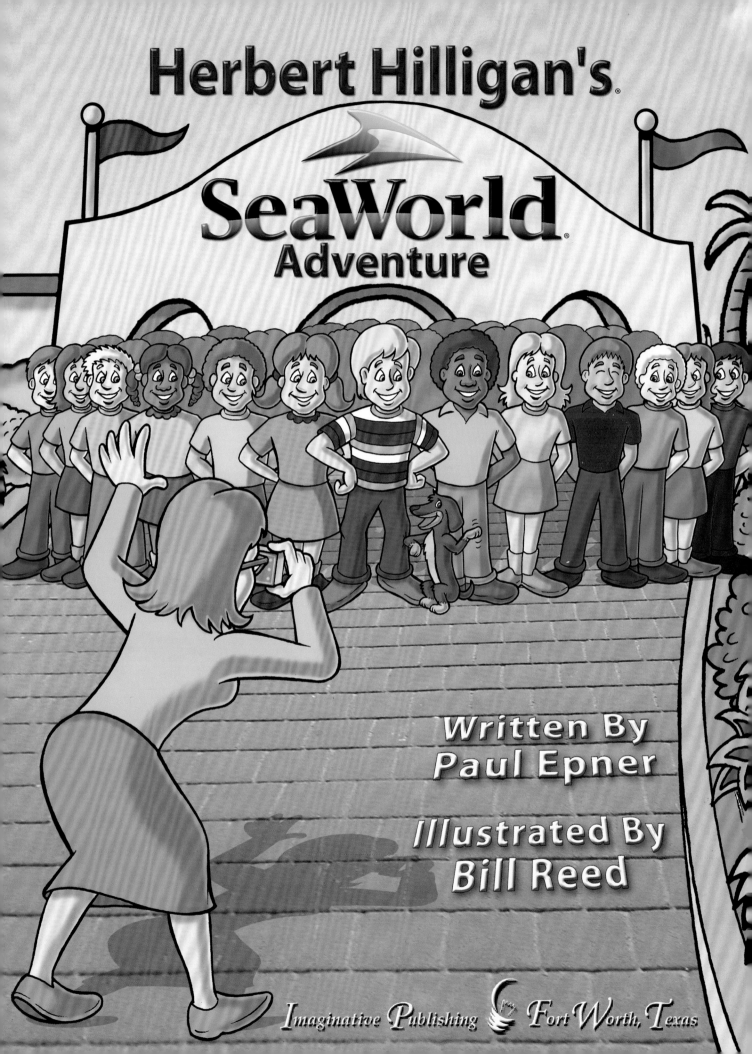

Herbert Hilligan's
SeaWorld Adventure

Written By
Paul Epner

Illustrated By
Bill Reed

Imaginative Publishing 🖋 *Fort Worth, Texas*

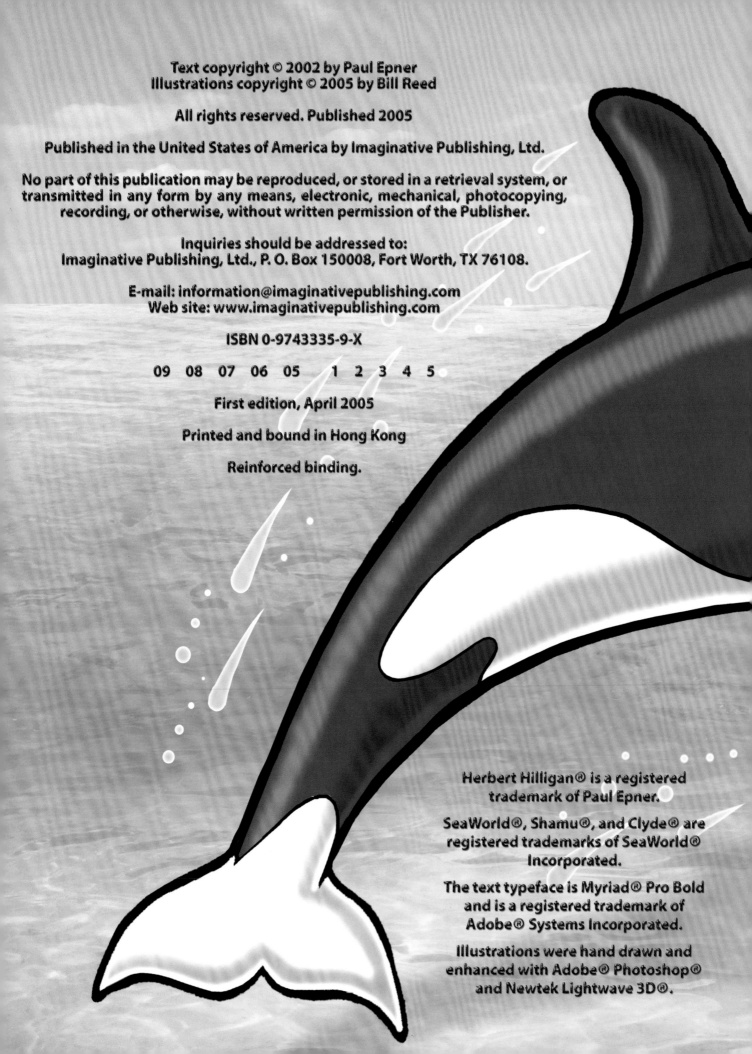

Published in the United States of America by Imaginative Publishing, Ltd.

Inquiries should be addressed to:
Imaginative Publishing, Ltd., P. O. Box 150008, Fort Worth, TX 76108.

E-mail: information@imaginativepublishing.com
Web site: www.imaginativepublishing.com

ISBN 0-9743335-9-X

09   08   07   06   05   1   2   3   4   5

First edition, April 2005

Printed and bound in Hong Kong

Reinforced binding.

For Allison my baby, you're so sweet and smart
You're beautiful, you're kind, and you have a great heart.

And to Susan her mother, this proves it to me,
A child like this falls close to the tree.

– P. E.

In memory of my father
Major William Reed IV, U.S.A.F.
Thank you for teaching me to be the best.

– B. R.

The school day began as all his days did
For Herbert Hilligan, an average kid.

The school bus they rode held 2 in a seat,
And all 30 seats were almost complete.

At SeaWorld that day they learned about Clyde
Who was found on the beach, lying sick on his side.

The sea lion pup had eaten a bag
He mistook for a fish, which caused him to gag.

His health was improving from SeaWorld's fine care —
It was trash in the ocean that put him in there.

If 8 pounds of food is what a sea lion ate
For every 100 pounds of that sea lion's weight,

"Foreign objects" dropped into the seas
Can hurt ocean friends like a deadly disease.

Objects like coins, although they are cash,
Are harmful to sea life as if they were trash.

A sea lion eats fish and finds them quite yummy,
But unusual objects shouldn't enter his tummy.

Then a 500-pound sea lion would certainly eat
How many pounds of a tasty sea treat?

As he learned about sea life and all types of fish
Herbert wanted to help, so he made a small wish.

The wish Herbert made? To help life in the sea
By keeping all oceans completely trash-free.

If we all pick up trash each day of the year
It wouldn't be long till the oceans were clear.

There was much more to learn, much more to know,
So on to the penguins in their house of cold snow.

PENGUIN ENCOUNTER

So if Herbert picks up 2 pounds every day,
In 1 year of time, he's cleared how much away?

The chinstrap, the rockhopper, the king and gentoo
Are four types of penguins the class got to view.

And though the class saw a total of four,
The number of types are so many more.

These black and white birds don't travel the sky
But swim through the water and don't ever fly.

17 types of penguins exist
According to those who make up the list.

Most live in cold weather, but some like it hot
And spend all their lives in a warm desert spot.

SeaWorld penguins find their housing quite nice
For a snow machine keeps them cooled down with ice.

If the class got to view a total of 4
The number of types is how many more?

As the class watched the penguins waddle about
The snow machine broke — it completely went out!

So in front of his teacher and classmates from school,
Herbert tossed out his lunchbox — the coolest of cool.

The lunchbox became a snow cone machine
Churning out ice that looked pure and clean.

The snow cone machine made ice really quick.
It made 10 pounds per hour, which was great fun to lick.

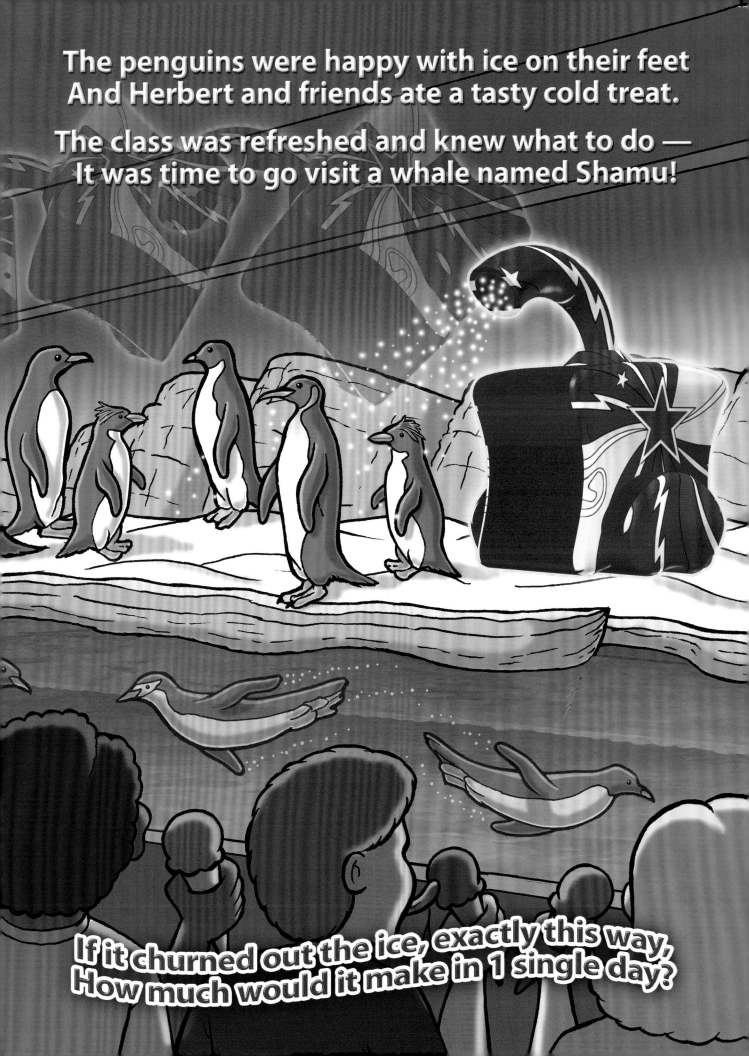

The penguins were happy with ice on their feet
And Herbert and friends ate a tasty cold treat.

The class was refreshed and knew what to do —
It was time to go visit a whale named Shamu!

If it churned out the ice, exactly this way,
How much would it make in 1 single day?

Killer whales like Shamu share a big family tree.
They're the largest type dolphins you'll ever see.

Shamu's not a fish and doesn't have scales
He's a mammal like us and like other "toothed whales."

Whales nurse their small babies and give them live birth
Like all mammals do that inhabit the earth.

5 tons in all is the weight of Shamu
This is a fact which is actually true.

Killer whales are warm-blooded and only breathe air,
And when they are young they even have hair.

To fill up his lungs with air from the sky
Shamu often "breaches" or jumps really high.

The jump that he makes with each single breach
Causes water to splash with a very long reach.

If 2,000 pounds equals exactly 1 ton
Your answer would be how many pounds when you're done?

So when Shamu splashed 'round in his big comfy pool
Herbert tossed out his lunchbox — the coolest of cool.

It became an umbrella in the blink of an eye
And kept Herbert's teacher warm, safe, and dry.

When Shamu catches air, he comes down with a crash
And 100 gallons spill out with his splash.

As Shamu waved 'bye with his "flukes"(that's his tail)
The class went to learn of another "toothed whale."

If Shamu makes 2 jumps each hour per day,
In 10 days of time, he'd splash how much away?

Dolphins, porpoises, and beluga whales too,
Are also toothed whales just like Shamu.

When dolphins must swim where there isn't much light
They cannot depend on their keen sense of sight.

To find things in water, or to help "navigate",
Dolphins are able to "echolocate."

A sound which takes 9 seconds to travel through air
Takes 2 seconds in water if you look to compare.

When they can't use their eyes and it's dark all around
Dolphins find things by using a sound.

They send out small noises that sound like a "click."
Bats and toothed whales share this sound-making trick.

As the sounds echo back, the dolphin can "read"
The size of an object, its shape and its speed.

For a 4-second sound in the ocean below
This same sound in air would take how long to go?

The class was now ready to go see a shark
In its watery habitat built in the park.

But before moving on, the teacher took roll,
And found that the class wasn't quite whole.

One student was missing, where could he be?
It was time to use sound to help Herbert see.

Class Roll
Herbert
Liz
Paul
George Ann
Mark
Mildred
Billy

Of the 25 students who made up the whole
All the girls could be counted when the teacher took roll.

As dolphins find things by using a sound
Herbert would use it to look all around.

The next thing he did made his classmates drool
As he threw out his lunchbox — the coolest of cool.

It became a huge truck, complete with a bell
That rang to announce there was ice cream to sell.

When the class is complete, there's 10 boys in the group
So what fraction are girls who make up this troop?

As they rode through the park the kids started to scream,
"Come and pig out on some tasty ice cream!"

The one missing student whom no one could see
Heard the bell ring and jumped up with glee.

He screamed with excitement and ran all around —
As he yelled for the ice cream, Herbert followed the sound.

The wheels on the truck go round and round
Completing a circle each 5 feet of ground.

Herbert "read" the loud sounds and used them to find
The one single student who'd been left behind.

Just as toothed whales use sound to locate,
Herbert did this to find his classmate.

And now that the student was finally back,
Everyone rested and had a cold snack.

If the ice cream truck drives 1,000 feet,
How many circles will each wheel complete?

They finished their ice cream and were ready to go,
When they heard a scared parent yell out: "OH, NO!"

"OH, NO!" the mom yelled as her hands lost their grip
And her kids in their stroller took a fast, scary trip.

Herbert thought quickly — he made a fast dash
To prevent a disaster and avoid a big crash.

The stroller rolled toward the sea lion pool,
So up went his lunchbox — the coolest of cool.

The stroller rolled fast, just 3 seconds to go
Down the small hill to the sea lions below.

It happened so fast, in a mind-blowing scene,
As the lunchbox became a huge trampoline.

The kids in the stroller were quiet and calm
As the trampoline bounced them all back to their mom.

The babies inside did not make a peep;
The triplets were quiet and all stayed asleep.

Coming back up the hill took twice as much time,
So how long in all did they roll down and climb?

Off went the class, and young Herbert, too,
To see all the sharks and learn something new.

Herbert studied the sharks with all of his class
And watched how they moved behind the clear glass.

He learned more that day than he had from his book
But felt he should have a much closer look.

Over 400,000 in the shark's swimming pool
Is the number of gallons they use to keep cool.

He hurled up his lunchbox — the coolest of cool —
And it landed inside the shark swimming pool.

Like the color and shape of a red jellybean,
The lunchbox became a cool submarine.

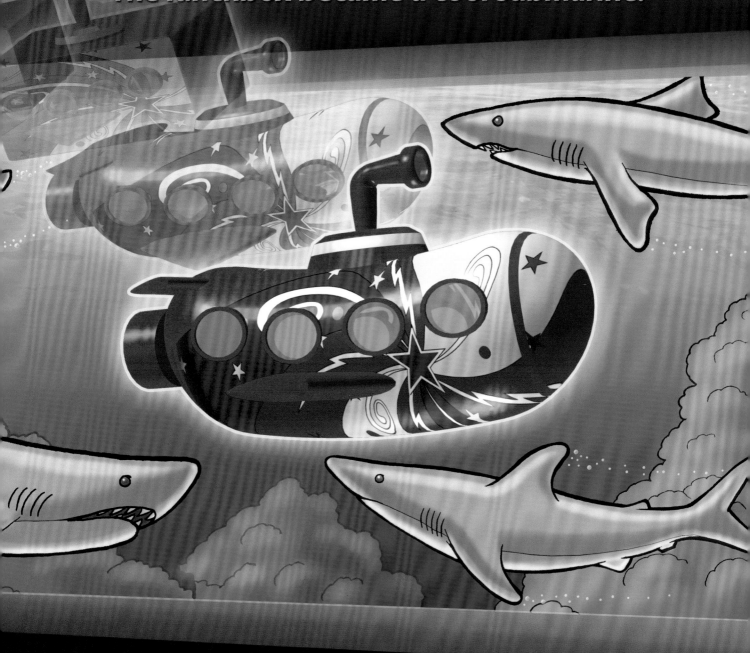

If Shamu's big pool is 5 times that much
How many gallons does he have to touch?

Herbert swam with the sharks, which gave him some thrills.
He noticed their fins, their teeth, and their gills.

And like all the fish that inhabit the sea,
That is what all sharks happen to be.

If 12 of 400 species of sharks
Swim around comfortably at SeaWorld's fine parks,

All sharks are fish and not mammals like whales,
For fish don't breathe air and are covered with scales.

Unlike most fish made of bones and a skeleton,
Sharks have cartilage — like really stiff gelatin.

It flexes and bends like your ears or your nose
And expands with the shark as its big body grows.

Of all the world's sharks in the oceans and seas
SeaWorld theme parks have what fraction of these?

As Herbert continued his submarine ride
He saw the sharks' mouths up close and inside.

The teeth that he saw were as sharp as a knife.
Thirty thousand can be lost in a single shark's life.

How much money do you think it would cost
If the tooth fairy came for each tooth that was lost?

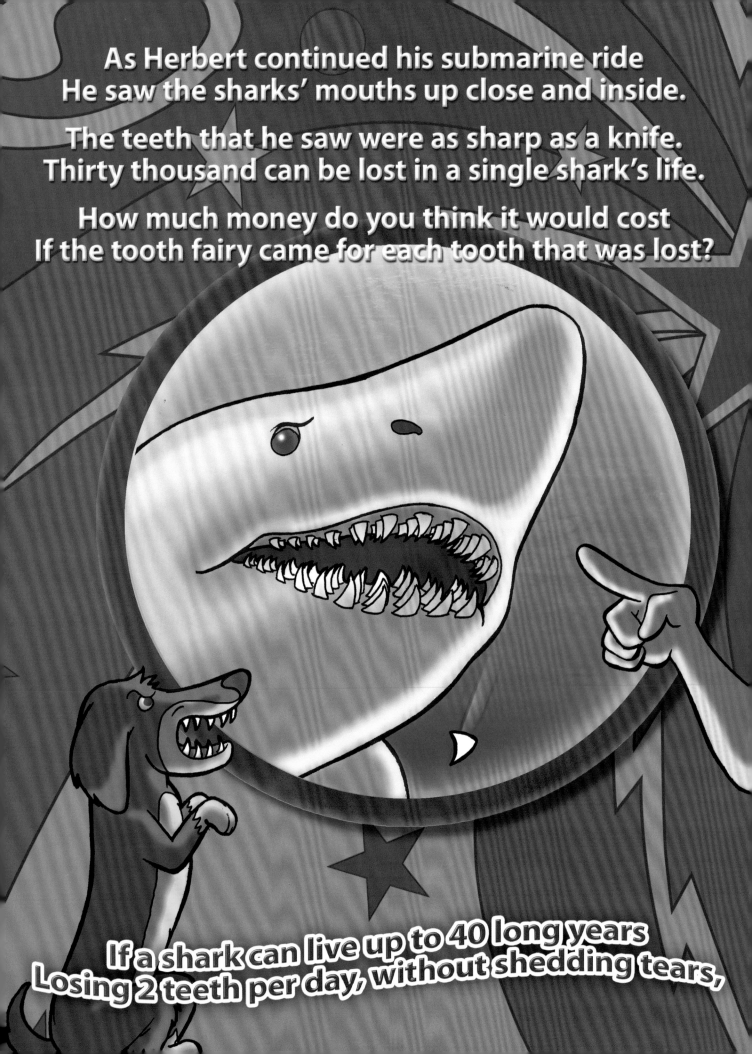

If a shark can live up to 40 long years
Losing 2 teeth per day, without shedding tears,

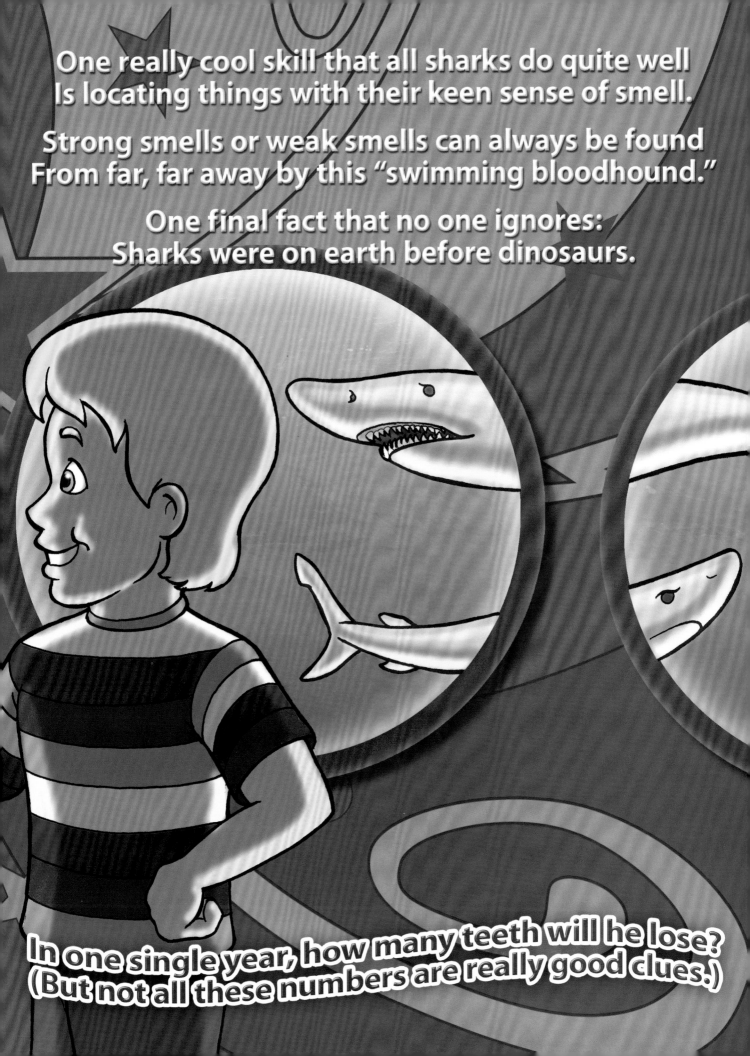

They wanted to see their friend once again
And check on his health in his watery den.

So off they all went to the sea lion pool,
Along with young Herbert and the coolest of cool.

A sea lion's weight, divided by 20,
Is the amount that he eats, which is really quite plenty.

Sea lions, walrus, and all harbor seals
Are called pinnipeds, and they like fishy meals.

As visitors bought fish for each pinniped
The sea lions awaited their turn to be fed.

But someone was planning to make a small wish
And was NOT getting ready to throw in a fish.

If 400 pounds is one sea lion's weight
How much do you think that sea lion ate?

But one little girl was ready to throw
A small, shiny coin to the sea lions below.

Herbert remembered the facts he'd been taught
About how Clyde was injured at the time he was caught:

This huge wishing well was 2 feet in height
And could hold many coins, to Herbert's delight.

"This sea lion pup had eaten a bag
He mistook for a fish, which caused him to gag."

"Objects like coins, although they are cash,
Are harmful to sea life as if they were trash."

Herbert tossed his red lunchbox — the coolest of cool —
So it landed away from the sea lion pool.

It quickly changed form and looked really swell —
The lunchbox became a huge wishing well!

If 16 stacked coins equal one inch in all
How many would stack in a huge well this tall?

So that one little girl with her shiny, round cash
Threw her coin in the well where it made a small splash.

And when the park visitors saw what she'd done,
They all did the same, one after one.

Quarters and nickels, pennies and dimes
All were thrown down in the well many times.

Even Herbert threw money and made a small wish
To help all the sea life and all types of fish.

So the class said good-bye to the sea lions below
And the field trip was over; it was time now to go.

If 10 of each coin were thrown down below
How much money did this well have to show?

They returned to their school, having learned a whole bunch.
Herbert opened his lunchbox, but where was his lunch?

His chocolate milk, cupcakes, and P.B. & J.
Were buried in cash from his journey that day!

Herbert honored his wish with this newly found wealth
To help all the sea life maintain their good health.

For 7 straight days, Herbert decided to pay
With the wishing well money, he DOUBLED each day.

He donated his money to help life in the sea
And to keep all the oceans completely trash-free.

And another day ended as all his days did
For Herbert Hilligan — an average kid.

Just an average day for Herbert at school
And his magical lunchbox — the coolest of cool.

If $400 came in on day one
What sum did he donate, once he was done?

If you like mathematics and sea animals, too,
Then this picture book is precisely for you.

Throughout this cool book, there's math to be done,
Whether easy or challenging, all of it's fun.

Multiply, add, divide, and subtract —
Make sure that your answers are correct and exact.

As you work through these problems, using your math
You should always consider there's more than one path.

The way that you solve it, the work that you do,
Can be different from others, if it makes sense to you.

If you need some advice as you read through this book,
Teachers and parents are a good place to look.

Math problem-solving is something I say
Happens in life, everywhere, everyday.

Learn to solve problems, listen in school.
Hard-working students are "the coolest of cool."

The school bus they rode held 2 in a seat,
And all 30 seats were almost complete.
But 3 of the seats held only 1,
So how many people were ready for fun?

Answer: 57 people

Step 1

$$
\begin{array}{r}
30 \\
\times\ 2 \\
\hline
60
\end{array}
$$

Step 2

$$
\begin{array}{r}
3 \\
\times\ 1 \\
\hline
3
\end{array}
$$

Step 3

$$
\begin{array}{r}
60 \\
-\ 3 \\
\hline
57
\end{array}
$$

If 8 pounds of food is what a sea lion ate
For every 100 pounds of that sea lion's weight,
Then a 500-pound sea lion would certainly eat
How many pounds of a tasty sea treat?

Answer: 40 pounds

Food	8	16	24	32	40
Weight	100	200	300	400	500

If we all pick up trash each day of the year
It wouldn't be long till the oceans were clear.

So if Herbert picks up 2 pounds every day,
In 1 year of time, he's cleared how much away?

Answer: 730 pounds of trash
Hint: 1 year = 365 days

$$
\begin{array}{r}
365 \\
\times2 \\
\hline
730
\end{array}
\qquad \text{or} \qquad
\begin{array}{r}
365 \\
+365 \\
\hline
730
\end{array}
$$

17 types of penguins exist
According to those who make up the list.

If the class got to view a total of 4
The number of types is how many more?

Answer: 13 more types

$$
\begin{array}{r}
17 \\
-4 \\
\hline
13
\end{array}
$$

The snow cone machine made ice really quick.
It made 10 pounds per hour, which was great fun to lick.
If it churned out the ice, exactly this way,
How much would it make in 1 single day?

Answer: 240 pounds of ice
Hint: 1 single day = 24 hours

$$
\begin{array}{r}
24 \\
\times\ 10 \\
\hline
00 \\
+\ 240 \\
\hline
240
\end{array}
$$

5 tons in all is the weight of Shamu
This is a fact which is actually true.
If 2,000 pounds equals exactly 1 ton
Your answer would be how many pounds when you're done?

Answer: 10,000 pounds

$$
\begin{array}{r}
2,000 \\
\times\qquad 5 \\
\hline
10,000
\end{array}
$$

When Shamu catches air, he comes down with a crash
And 100 gallons spill out with his splash.
If Shamu makes 2 jumps each hour per day,
In 10 days of time, he'd splash how much away?
Answer: 48,000 gallons of water

Step 1
```
  100
X   2
  200
```

Step 2
```
   200
X   24
   800
+ 4000
 4,800
```

Step 3
```
  4,800
X    10
  0000
+ 48000
 48,000
```

A sound which takes 9 seconds to travel through air
Takes 2 seconds in water if you look to compare.
For a 4-second sound in the ocean below
This same sound in air would take how long to go?
Answer: 18 seconds to travel through the air

Seconds in air	9	18
Seconds in water	2	4

Of the 25 students who made up the whole
All the girls could be counted when the teacher took roll.
When the class is complete, there's 10 boys in the group
So what fraction are girls who make up this troop?

Answer: 15/25 of the students are girls

$$\frac{25}{25} - \frac{10}{25} = \frac{15}{25}$$

The wheels on the truck go round and round
Completing a circle each 5 feet of ground.
If the ice cream truck drives 1,000 feet,
How many circles will each wheel complete?

Answer: 200 circles each

```
      200
  5 )1000
    −10
      00
    − 00
      00
    − 00
       0
```

The stroller rolled fast, just 3 seconds to go
Down the small hill to the sea lions below.
Coming back up the hill took twice as much time,
So how long in all did they roll down and climb?

Answer: 9 seconds

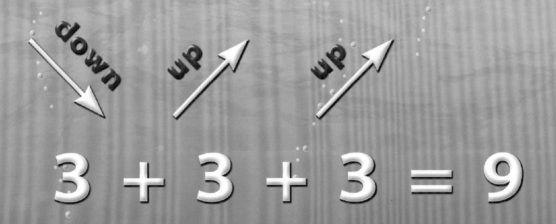

$$3 + 3 + 3 = 9$$

Over 400,000 in the shark's swimming pool
Is the number of gallons they use to keep cool.
If Shamu's big pool is 5 times that much
How many gallons does he have to touch?

Answer: 2,000,000 gallons

```
    400,000
  X       5
  _____
  2,000,000
```

If 12 of 400 species of sharks
Swim around comfortably at SeaWorld's fine parks,
Of all the world's sharks in the oceans and seas
SeaWorld theme parks have what fraction of these?

Answer: 3/100 or 3%

$$\frac{12}{400} \div \frac{4}{4} = \frac{3}{100} \quad \text{or} \quad 3\%$$

If a shark can live up to 40 long years
Losing 2 teeth per day, without shedding tears,
In one single year, how many teeth will he lose?
(But not all these numbers are really good clues.)

Answer: 730 teeth in one year
Hint: 1 year = 365 days

$$\begin{array}{r} 365 \\ \times\ 2 \\ \hline 730 \end{array} \quad \text{or} \quad \begin{array}{r} 365 \\ +365 \\ \hline 730 \end{array}$$

A sea lion's weight, divided by 20,
Is the amount that he eats, which is really quite plenty.

If 400 pounds is one sea lion's weight
How much do you think that sea lion ate?

Answer: 20 pounds of food

$$
\begin{array}{r}
20 \\
20\,\overline{)\,400} \\
-40 \\
\hline
00 \\
-\,00 \\
\hline
0
\end{array}
$$

This huge wishing well was 2 feet in height
And could hold many coins, to Herbert's delight.

If 16 stacked coins equal one inch in all
How many would stack in a huge well this tall?

Answer: 384 coins

Step 1

$$
\begin{array}{r}
16 \\
\times\ 12 \\
\hline
32 \\
+\ 160 \\
\hline
192
\end{array}
$$

Step 2

$$
\begin{array}{r}
192 \\
\times\ \ 2 \\
\hline
384
\end{array}
$$

Quarters and nickels, pennies and dimes
All were thrown down in the well many times.
If 10 of each coin were thrown down below
How much money did this well have to show?

Answer: $4.10

Quarters
10
X .25
50
+200
2.50

Dimes
10
X .10
00
+ 100
1.00

Nickels
10
X .05
50
+000
.50

Pennies
10
X .01
10
+000
.10

2.50
1.00
.50
+ .10
4.10

For 7 straight days, Herbert decided to pay
With the wishing well money, he DOUBLED each day.
If $400 came in on day one
What sum did he donate, once he was done?

Answer: $50,800

Day	1	2	3	4	5	6	7
Money	400	800	1,600	3,200	6,400	12,800	25,600

25,600
12,800
6,400
3,200
1,600
800
+ 400
50,800

My classmates and I enjoyed our day at SeaWorld sooo much, we decided to help all the animals in the ocean. Now you can, too.

The SeaWorld & Busch Gardens Conservation Fund donates to wildlife conservation projects around the world. They're helping study penguins in the Galapagos Islands and looking at where Pacific Loggerhead Sea Turtles go when they're swimming around Japan and following Right Whales in Florida.

SeaWorld and Busch Gardens parks are part of the Busch Entertainment Corporation, and they've been helping to conserve, rescue and study animals for more than 40 years. They have assisted more than 5,000 stranded, ill, orphaned or injured animals in the past ten years.

To find out more about this great way to help the animals of the world, visit swbg-conservationfund.org. All those coins really add up!

Herbert